No T.REX in the Library

by Toni Buzzeo

illustrated by Sachiko Yoshikawa

SCHOLASTIC INC.
New York Toronto London Auckland
Sydney Mexico City New Delhi Hong Kong

To **Emma**, with love and thanks for her perfect **Eureka!** moment
—T. B.

To Mela, Max, and Maya—S. Y.

ISBN 978-0-545-35790-6

12 11 10 9 8 7 6 5 4 3 2 1   11 12 13 14 15 16/0

Printed in the U.S.A.   08

First Scholastic printing, March 2011

Book design by Debra Sfetsios
The text for this book is set in Softie.
The illustrations for this book are rendered in mixed media
(colored pencils, gouache, markers, acrylics, soft pastels, and collage).

It's Tuesday morning in the library.

"ROAR!"

Tess is out of control.

"TIME OUT!"

Mommy shouts.

"No beastie behavior in the library."

Tess **snarls.**

She **snorts.**

"Just ten quiet minutes,
Little Beastie," says Mommy.
"And then I'll be back for you."

BAM!

Books tumble,

topple,

flop on the floor.

"OOPS!" Tess says. **"The books . . ."**

"ROAR!"

She gasps and grins.
She grips a claw.

And then . . .

T. Rex zips through the children's room.
Tess **bumps** along on his back.

"**Yee-haw!**"

Tess cheers.

Readers scatter in the wild clatter
of the history books tumbling down.

"Watch out!" Tess shouts.

"The books . . ."

Now knights in gleaming armor
lay siege,
hoisting their flags
and wheeling their steeds.

"Charge on,"
Tess trumpets.

T. Rex **tilts** and **whirls** through the door.

"Wait!" Tess shouts.

"The books . . ."

Water **spills** as the story pit fills with fish and aquarium treasures.

Orcas spout high.
Swordfish, jellies,
and squid reel by
the knights doing
synchronized swimming.

T. Rex **cannonballs** through them all . . .

. . . and bubbles up guarding the treasure.
A swashbuckling pirate surfaces nearby,
brandishing a hook for a hand.

"Arrr!
Return me booty, scurvy dog."

T. Rex escapes through the
Wild West display,
stomping past books on the floor.

"Be careful!" Tess cries.

"The books . . ."

Wild West

A posse of cowboys **gallops up** off the pages, their lassos **atwirl** overhead.

T. Rex **reels** through sagebrush and books. **Cattle stampede at his heels.**

"Take care!" Tess pleads.

"The books . . ."

T. Rex **thrashes**

and

trashes

Grabbing masses and mounds and

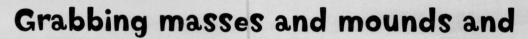

he builds

the
shelves.

mountains of books,

an escape to the stars.

Earth & Science

From M to Mars—

"Please don't," Tess whispers.

From J to Jupiter—

"No! No!" Tess exclaims.

From S to Saturn—

"Please stop.

They're ripping!" she begs.

And on to . . .

RIIIIIIII

"TIME OUT!" Tess shouts.

"You're out of control!" Tess growls.

"No beastie behavior
with my library books."

T. Rex **fidgets.**
He **fusses.**
He **flings** out his tail.

BAM!

Books tumble,

topple,

flop

on the floor.

"ROAR?"

Tess **pushes** and
pokes him.

She presses him
into his book.

"Just ten quiet minutes, Little Beastie,"

Tess whispers.

"And then I'll be back for you. . . ."